TINY HAMSTER IS A GIANT MONSTER

JOEL JENSEN, JOSEPH MATSUSHIMA & AMY MATSUSHIMA

SIMON & SCHUSTER BOOKS FOR YOUNG READERS
New York   London   Toronto   Sydney   New Delhi

THIS BOOK IS DEDICATED TO REJECTED IDEAS AND THE WORD "NO." THIS BOOK IS ALSO DEDICATED TO OUR PARENTS AND THE CHILDHOOD PETS THEY ENDURED.

SIMON & SCHUSTER BOOKS FOR YOUNG READERS
An imprint of Simon & Schuster Children's Publishing Division
1230 Avenue of the Americas, New York, New York 10020
Text and images copyright © 2015 by Joel Jensen, Joseph Matsushima, and Amy Matsushima
Supplemental images of burrito, cupcake, and sitting hamster body copyright © 2015 by Thinkstock.com
Production art direction by Abigail Childs
Retouching by We Monsters

SIMON & SCHUSTER BOOKS FOR YOUNG READERS is a trademark of Simon & Schuster, Inc.
For information about special discounts for bulk purchases, please contact Simon & Schuster Special Sales at 1-866-506-1949 or business@simonandschuster.com.
The Simon & Schuster Speakers Bureau can bring authors to your live event. For more information or to book an event, contact the Simon & Schuster Speakers Bureau at 1-866-248-3049 or visit our website at www.simonspeakers.com.
Book design by Lucy Ruth Cummins
The text for this book is set in Avenir.
The illustrations for this book are rendered from video footage.
Manufactured in the United States of America
0415 PCH
10 9 8 7 6 5 4 3 2 1
CIP data for this book is available from the Library of Congress.
ISBN 978-1-4814-5110-9
ISBN 978-1-4814-5111-6 (eBook)

first edition

ONE CLOUDY DAY, Tiny Hamster went out to find a bite to eat. Tiny Hamster was always hungry, you see, and today was no different.

A storm was coming, but Tiny Hamster could only think about food. His tummy grumbled and mumbled and tumbled around inside him.

That's when he saw it—a bright orange tub full of neon green ooze. It looked delicious!

Just as Tiny Hamster's tiny tongue touched the ooze, a bolt of lightning streaked down from the sky, swallowing him up in brightness.

TINY HAMSTER'S MOUTH FELT NUMB.

HIS EYES WENT WIDE.

HIS EARS TWITCHED.

HIS TUMMY GRUMBLED AND MUMBLED AND TUMBLED AROUND INSIDE HIM.

HE FELT HIMSELF INFLATE LIKE A BIG BALLOON THAT KEPT GETTING BIGGER!

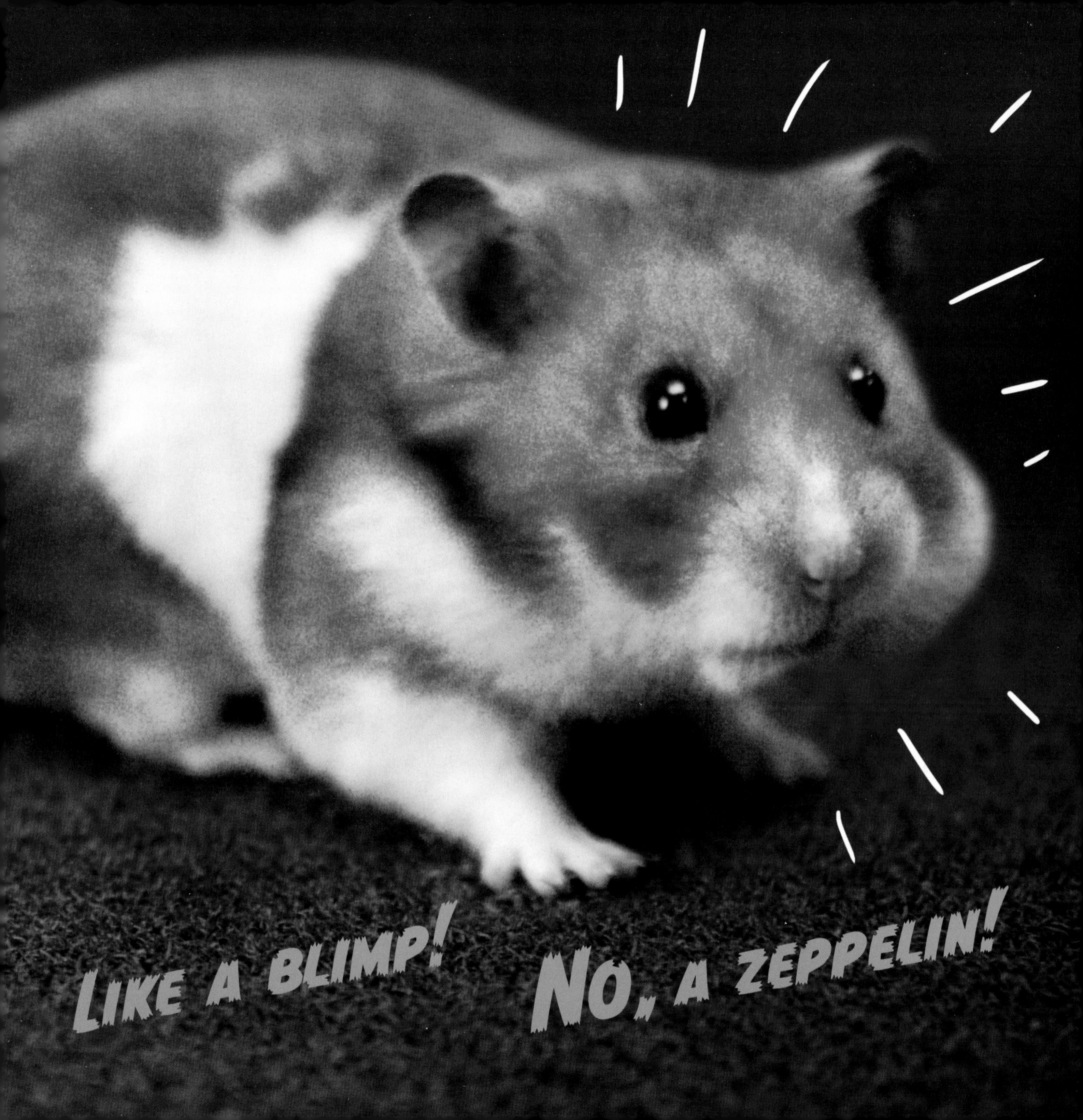
LIKE A BLIMP!
NO, A ZEPPELIN!

His paws grew huge and clumsy, and he could feel sharp spikes spring out of his back. Then he turned *green*!

Tiny Hamster had become a giant monster.
Worse yet, he was even hungrier than before.

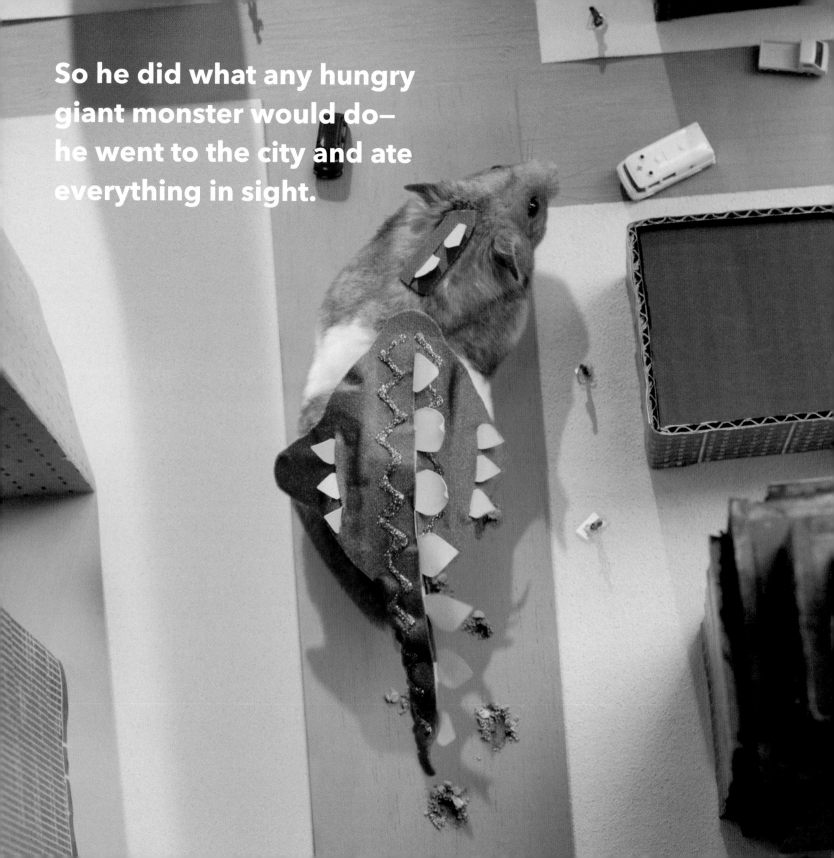

So he did what any hungry giant monster would do–
he went to the city and ate everything in sight.

He chomped on some trees.

They were very good.

A train rolled past, and he ate it. It was tasty.

He spotted a
billboard
and gobbled it
right up.
Yum!

**Tiny Hamster the Giant Monster
took a bite right out of a building.**

He nibbled another one,
but it toppled over. Whoops!

Tiny Hamster the Giant Monster was still hungry. He climbed right up a skyscraper to see what else there was to eat.

Helicopters *thuck-thuck-thuck*ed through the air, hovering around his head.

**Tiny Hamster the Giant Monster
scarfed them straight out of the sky!**

One helicopter carried a giant orange tub full of green ooze. It looked delicious, but the helicopter began to fly away.

Tiny Hamster the Giant
Monster followed it.

Soon the delicious green ooze was within reach!

Tiny Hamster the Giant Monster could already taste it.

Just as the giant monster's giant tongue touched the ooze, a bolt of lightning streaked down from the sky, swallowing him up in brightness.

HIS MOUTH FELT NUMB.

HIS EYES
WENT WIDE.

HIS EARS
TWITCHED.

HIS TUMMY GRUMBLED AND MUMBLED AND
TUMBLED AROUND INSIDE HIM.

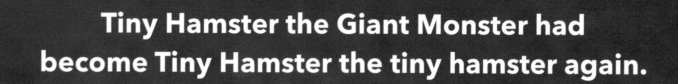

Tiny Hamster the Giant Monster had become Tiny Hamster the tiny hamster again.

Better yet, he was finally full.

Now it was time for dessert!